Shiverses

Spine-chilling Poesies

W. J. Manares

Ukiyoto Publishing

All global publishing rights are held by

Ukiyoto Publishing

Published in 2023

Content Copyright © W. J. Manares

ISBN 9789360164225

*All rights reserved.
No part of this publication may be reproduced, transmitted, or stored in a retrieval system, in any form by any means, electronic, mechanical, photocopying, recording or otherwise, without the prior permission of the publisher.*

The moral rights of the authors have been asserted.

This is a work of fiction. Names, characters, businesses, places, events, locales, and incidents are either the products of the author's imagination or used in a fictitious manner. Any resemblance to actual persons, living or dead, or actual events is purely coincidental.

This book is sold subject to the condition that it shall not by way of trade or otherwise, be lent, resold, hired out or otherwise circulated, without the publisher's prior consent, in any form of binding or cover other than that in which it is published.

www.ukiyoto.com

Dedication

To Arianne, the girl who scared the shit out of me

WARNING: This is a Daytime Book!

These poems will scare the shit out of you!

Another one-of-a-kind collection from the "self-proclaimed" most talented and prolific Ukiyoto author and multi-awarded poet of his generation, W. J. Manares

SHIVERSES
Spine-chilling Poesies

Book Cover Art: gl_die/gladrvr/Gladie

Contents

THE WOODS	1
WITCHING HOUR	2
LOUP-GAROU	3
THE SUCCUBUS	4
LAMIA	5
INVISIBLES	6
THE WITCH	7
CORPSE-EATER	8
JUST ANOTHER ASWANG	9
HAUNTED	10
LADY IN WHITE	11
CORVUS CORAX	12
HORSE POWER	13
LADY HUKLUBAN	14
DUSK	15
THE KATAW	16
DANCING LADY	17
TREE-DWELLING KAPRE	18
DWARVES	19
FOREST CREATURES	20

SIRENADE	21
DEMONS-TRATION	22
PSYCHO	23
LADY IN CRIMSON	24
THE BATIBAT	25
COWARDLY BRAVE	26
REAPER-TOIRE	27
SCAN-DOLL	28
CLOWN	29
THE UNBORN	30
THE MANANANGGAL	31
RED MOON	32
THE MANGILAW	33
CREATURES OF THE DEEP	34
EERIE	35
BELDAME	36
SHARED STORIES, TATTLED TALES	37
THE UNKNOWN	38
THE SIGBIN	39
GORGEOUS GORGON	40
LEVIATHAN	41
DEVIL LIVED	42

COUNT	43
THE RAVEN	44
WEREWOLF	45
HADES	46
NESSY	47
HYDRA	48
LILITH	49
INTO THE WOODLAND	50
About the Author	51

THE WOODS

Into the woods
full of spook
the ambiance of horror
with a little bit of sorrow

the crows flew
the eerie atmosphere grew
and the fear outgrew
welcome to the woods, my dear crew

WITCHING HOUR

Spooky tales at night
monsters' delight
the red moon
fear will bloom

the curtains danced
taking the chance
to scare that someone
who's still awaked at one

LOUP-GAROU

The Werewolf howls
its stomach growls
a sign of hunger
for the savage hunter

He searched for victims
old or someone younger
fat or slim
till' he's satisfied, he will slaughter

THE SUCCUBUS

Long hair, red lips
and her hypnotizing kiss,
fair skin, angelic voice
Men's heart will rejoice

Her red lips will peck a kiss
red mark on the cheeks
will pull you into a deep sleep
she's the woman and a creep

LAMIA

Creatures with pale skin
red eyes burning
black and slim
and fangs that can sting

Blood is what they drink
and they can kill you, even when you blink
"stay away" is my advice
or witness your demise

INVISIBLES

You can't see them,
but can feel them,
you can't hear them,
when they're screaming.

Showing themselves in your dream,
and there they'll make you scream,
never ever joke about it,
Lost ghosts and evil spirits.

THE WITCH

Full moon tonight,
Someone's delight,
It's cold and dark,
Hear the dogs bark,

A lady in a broomstick,
I wonder if she's sick,
Wandering for her supper,
Are you willing to suffer?

CORPSE-EATER

Corpses are its main dish,
disliking meat or fish,
Eager to eat someone deceased,
Recorded stolen corpses, increased.

A dark buddy,
it's odor hated by everybody,
you'd better pray, for someone's body,
because this "Balbal" isn't just somebody.

JUST ANOTHER ASWANG

A monster known for killing
newborns that are sleeping
in the pregnant woman's womb
soon it'll be the baby's tomb

It's long tongue that can reach this new flesh,
preferring something fresh,
a fetus inside her belly,
the monster sees it as sweet jelly.

HAUNTED

A room filled with darkness,
consisting emptiness,
Listen to someone's cry,
reaching the sky,

A lady scared and lonely,
whining for justice,
in the empty space she's staring,
a smile creeping out of her lips.

LADY IN WHITE

An evil spirit,
that lurks at night,
fear of people is her delight,
and her specialty is fright

Calling out your name,
sudden appearance is her game,
You may call her "white lady",
better run, veteran, she's in the alley

CORVUS CORAX

Black feathers, red eyes,
a sign of demise,
soaring in the sky,
the devil's spy

Full of wrath,
a part of witchcraft,
Evil intents in the air,
Ravens abruptly appear

HORSE POWER

Deep in the woods resting,
horse-headed humanoids,
there's a lot of them to count,
Chiron's lost relatives

Deep in the woods, a colony,
you'll witness a wedding ceremony,
of mythical creatures,
called "Tikbalangs" by the community

LADY HUKLUBAN

In a house that's fancy,
lives a lonely lady named Hukluban
she'll welcome you inside,
But you must be polite

or else,
she'll make you her dinner,
innerts, flavors enriched,
cadaver in the ditch

But still in no time you'll become a dish,
Still you'll surely perish,
Lady Hukluban is more than a witch,
Eating humans, her greatest wish

DUSK

Evening is arriving,
a sign of mourning,
it's a bad news, it's a warning,
you must be praying

Monsters that lurks at night,
Demons in sight,
spreading fright,
you'll never win without a fight

THE KATAW

Beautiful hair,
skin so fair,
eyes that's sparkling,
her smile so charming

but never be fooled,
she sees you as food,
she's a sea creature, a mermaid,
you'd better be afraid

DANCING LADY

In the streets, see her dancing,
at night, everything's frightening,
stay away,
stay awake

A weird dance,
she'll notice you in a glance,
start running,
like a husky panting

TREE-DWELLING KAPRE

He is a smoker,
he is a lot taller,
living in a big tree,
away from the city

He is mysterious
yet everyone knows him,
ain't guapito but he's macho,
sometimes harmful and evil,
move slowly or just stay still

DWARVES

A colony of small people,
optimistic yet evil,
their voices are tiny,
they contain ferocity

you must never disturb them,
they will bring you mayhem,
they're ready to start a war,
it's them the dwarves

FOREST CREATURES

In the forest they live,
mystery-filled,
curiousity spreading,
rumors about them
we're shared

sometimes hostile,
some are good, some are vile,
you're in trouble if they want you,
they'll do everything to take you

SIRENADE

They sing the songs of the sea,
where, in the dark depths human can't see,
they'll hypnotize every human they see,
and then those people can't flee

They are truly full of beauty,
but they are deadly,
they are angelic,
but at the same time demonic

DEMONS-TRATION

They love spreading fear,
scatter in the atmosphere,
they are merciless,
and they are full of evil

In your dreams they'll meddle,
and do something devilish
never let you rest,
scare you at their best

Full of malice and hate,
will interfere with your fate,
they will make humans desperate,
consider them as a great threat

PSYCHO

Silence was covering the place,
it's dark and dangerous,
a murderer with an evil face,
merciless and murderous

He killed a lot,
and he will kill more,
old or newborn,
he is truly an eyesore

LADY IN CRIMSON

A lady with a crimson-stained dress,
full of sorrow and stress,
bloodshot eyes full of malice,
her soul cries for justice

Her lost soul wandered,
around the place where she was murdered,
her evil intents lies ahead,
because she was never been defended

THE BATIBAT

A fat lady
full of evil deeds,
she'll scare you as long as she wants,
in your nightmares you'll never be free

she's famous,
feared by everyone in their sleep,
she is ferocious,
she is the "Batibat"
responsible for sleep paralysis

COWARDLY BRAVE

Full moon at night,
cowards will be at fright,
something lurks in the shadows,
they will spread despair and sorrow

be brave,
because they will never hesitate,
to make your life a mess,
they will put you in distress

REAPER-TOIRE

Dark cloak, a skeleton,
holding a scythe
the escort,
he guides everyone,
to their last resort
that is death,
your very last companion,
the keeper, harvester of souls
also known as the Grim Reaper
join him in your final destination

SCAN-DOLL

Love a doll,
cuddly and sweet
gorgeous and adorable,
purchased by people, sometimes a gift
yet it can cause some trouble

Left behind
in a very dark room,
and there, fear will bloom,
evil will possess the empty shell,
scandalous creature from hell

CLOWN

A face full of powder,
a funny fellow of anger,
those red cheeks,
gave me the creeps

He acts foolish and deep,
but inside him is malice,
looks like a sheep
but he is truly devilish

He can make everyone smile
from lame jokes to magic tricks,
he is the jester
a total hit

THE UNBORN

There was a child,
or rather a baby,
that acts innocently,
but he is wild

He might be small,
but he can kill y'all,
ain't weak, wicked
he's vulnerable like you

THE MANANANGGAL

A lady who can separate her body,
at night everything will be bloody,
she is feared by everybody,
she can devour anybody

A true monster,
a certified man-eater,
her half body terrifies all,
her hunger for flesh is always there

RED MOON

The red moon at night,
brings fear and mayhem,
the air spreads panic,
everyone's hope had fallen

The red moon that shines
sends shiver to my spine,
it is a sign, for us to know,
that the light of hope will never glow

The red moon shows that,
hope will be lost
and it's the devil's warning,
that darkness will be reigning

THE MANGILAW

A savage hunter,
a merciless killer,
full of murderous intents,
and he'd kill to his heart's content

Pigman is what he's called,
he is rather wild or bold,
so do your best to hide,
or just stand and be terrified

CREATURES OF THE DEEP

Under the sea is their home, the unreached,
Down there in the deep cold waters,
some creatures lurk,
in different sizes,
with a manifestation of strength

creatures known by sailors of old,
as they spoke of it with fear,
the mariner's nightmare,
this tells us how terrifying
the sea could be

EERIE

Someone we can't see?
A presence,
Is it a ghost full of malice?
Or another victim of injustice?

This feeling tells me that,
There's someone I can't gaze at,
Somebody I can't grasp,
Not really good, is it bad?

BELDAME

An old woman who knows alchemy,
makes potion, chants and spells and can curse many,
she flies in the midnight air,
in search for child at fear

An instant trickster,
and she is known for bringing misery,
a lady full of cruelty,
witchcraft is her specialty

SHARED STORIES, TATTLED TALES

They thirst for blood, different blends,
And they crave for flesh,
monsters in urban legends,
their stories are still fresh
I want to hear tales like these!

People talk about them as time passes,
spooky tales shared for all ages,
the youngsters would fear,
but the stories of the young-at-hearts
are still fun to hear

THE UNKNOWN

creatures, entities
whatever you're calling them,
under your bed, inside the closet
they're terrible and causes alarm

They might be friendly, keep
but they're still scary, creep
don't ever think they're nice,
devils in disguise

THE SIGBIN

a twisted body,
walking awkwardly,
a walking contradiction
pet from other dimension
smells strangely,
seen by many

A body bent,
everyone catches
the unusual scent,
chupacbra of old,
a llama, a kangaroo
called "Sigbin" by a few

GORGEOUS GORGON

She is a victim of injustice,
A chalice full of malice,
one of the goddesses,
a true gorgeous temptress

Her hair covered in snakes,
she'll do whatever it takes,
to bring back her dignity,
punishing the guilty

The head covering, her protection,
also the sign of someone's violation,
Her name is Medusa,
the gorgon by Athena

LEVIATHAN

A sea monster that's what it is called,
big and long,
It rides with the ocean waves,
and sailors are what it craves

It has this slimy body,
feared by everybody,
It swims under the sea,
where no one can see

DEVIL LIVED

An evil spirit lurking around,
in this unfamiliar ground,
where he spreads his evil deeds,
this is a demon full of greed

You can say it is hostile,
and this creature is vile,
don't you dare interfere,
or else you'll taste fear

COUNT

A famous creature,
and a bloodsucker,
he's part of another
country's culture

full of mystery
archaic tale, old movie
count him as dangerous,
consider him as flagitious

THE RAVEN

Black feathers that fell,
a creature from hell,
its red eyes are intimidating,
the raven is soaring

Its soar is a sign or warning,
for something dangerous that's coming,
so you'd better be alert,
for this creature isn't just a bird

WEREWOLF

It stood in the center of the moon,
and howls in the cold night air,
it's a bad omen, cave canem
not just a simple dog

A man feared by humanity,
hiding himself from society,
the savage carnivore
Is there any cure?

HADES

god of the underworld,
a mighty lord,
dark and evil,
definitely, he will kill

Hades is the name
death and torture are his games
one of the Greek gods,
that will make you mad

In his world, land of no return
All your remains will burn
While you taste his wickedness
And his violent caress

NESSY

A sea shanty, a humungous creature,
it can gobble up a boat with full force,
In Lake Ness, a rumored monster,
Some see it floating in the river

A long body and slippery figure,
it's either a reptile, perhaps a carnivore
in those deep waters it hides,
and sometimes rises in the shadows

HYDRA

A demon of ambiguity,
with wide and slender body,
a huge Snake with great history,
a reptilian that brings agony

The demonic snake,
the nine-headed serpent
very dangerous and full of wrath,
Don't dare to trod the evil path